THIS
BUG!

By Sydney & Alyssa Holmes

We'll draw the bug,
YOU draw the rest!

*Dedicated to Nolan and to all of the kids
doing their part to flatten the curve.*

The grown-ups all say
here's a bug going 'round,

so we have to stay home where
we're safe and we're sound.

This bug he's not big,
he's one you can carry.
For young kids like me,
this bug's not as scary.

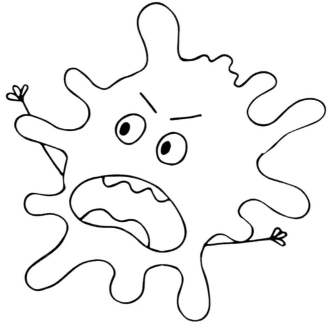

To some he's not nice,
he's got tricks up his sleeve,
so we'll stay in our house
and we'll try not to leave.

This bug he's **SO** famous,
he won't go away!
The grown-ups they speak
of him day after day.

On TV, at dinner,
on Facetime with friends...
when will the talk of
this bug **EVER** end?!

At first, it was fun -
no teachers, no rules,
no classroom, no homework,
no math and no school!

But wait just a minute!
f school comes to an end...

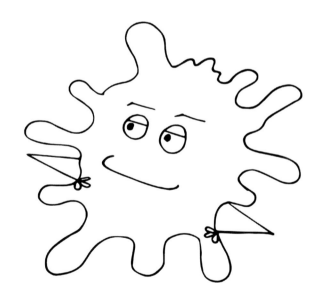

how am I supposed
to see all of my friends?

They'll stay at their home
and I'll stay at mine,
with grown-ups just washing
their hands **ALL** the time.

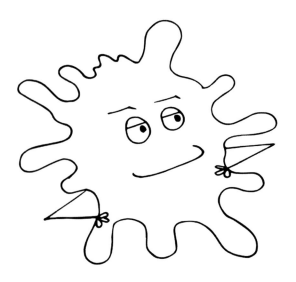

They say that my Grandpa
can't come out to play...
even my Grandma
stands 6 feet away.

This bug wants to ruin
all of my fun,
but this is a battle
that's **YET** to be won.

They say he's afraid
of our squeaky clean hands
and he can't move around
if we watch where we stand.

This bug wants us home
all alone by ourselves
with toilet paper filling
up all of our shelves.

What this bug doesn't know
is we're smarter than that.
We can make our homes fun
at the drop of a hat.

We'll build all the forts,
we'll read all the books,
we'll bake some fresh bread
and we'll learn how to cook.

And just when the grown-ups
think all the fun's through,
that's when us kids
know **JUST** what to do!

There's something inside us
that cannot be taught...

imagination can change things
in one single thought.

For the **HEROES** still fighting
this bug that's out there,
we'll do our part,
stay home,
show we care.

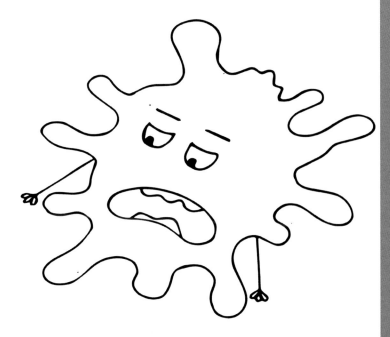

We'll make things and dream up
new ways to have fun
'till this bug's gone away...

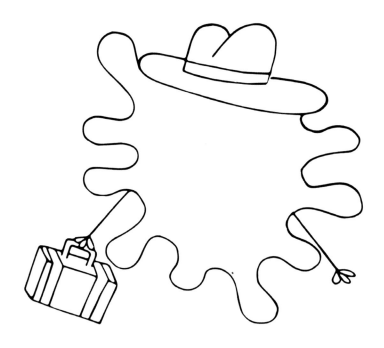

and the battle's been won!

Manufactured by Amazon.ca
Bolton, ON

12332171R00017

In times of uncertainty we have always relied on creative expression to get us through. We've written this book during an unprecedented time in human history and hope it acts as a tool for you to express your own unique perspective.

Sydney & Alyssa Holmes

ISBN 9798637582228

Social Cognition and Communication

Edited by

JOSEPH P. FORGAS
ORSOLYA VINCZE,
AND JÁNOS LÁSZLÓ

Psychology Press